Stephen Gammell

Once Upon MacDonald's Farm...

Aladdin Paperbacks

Aladdin Paperbacks
An imprint of Simon & Schuster
Children's Publishing Division
1230 Avenue of the Americas
New York, NY 10020

First Aladdin Paperbacks edition, 1990

10   9   8   7   6   5   4

Library of Congress Cataloging-in-Publication Data
Gammell, Stephen.
Once upon MacDonald's farm/Stephen Gammell. — 1st Aladdin Books ed.   p.   cm.
Summary: MacDonald tries farming with exotic circus animals but has better luck with his
neighbor's cow, horse, and chicken — or does he?
ISBN 0-689-71379-7
[1. Farm life — Fiction.   2. Animals — Fiction.   3. Humorous stories.]   I. Title.
[PZ7.G144On   1990]
[E]—dc20   89-17792   CIP   AC

To my dear One,
my family
and Sully...

While it is true that MacDonald had a farm...

it wasn't much of a farm,

and he had no animals.
None at all.

"I really must have some animals…"

So, he bought an elephant....

he also bought a baboon
and a lion.

In the morning, MacDonald and the elephant went out to the field...

to do the plowing.

Much later that afternoon,

there were still some chores
to be done.

MacDonald was weary, and went to bed early.

But while he slept, the animals
decided to leave. And did...

without a sound.

When MacDonald awoke, he had no animals...

but his neighbor offered
to help.

That evening, he sent over
a horse, a cow and a chicken.

MacDonald was thankful for his new animals.

So, after a good sleep and a healthy breakfast, he was eager to start work.

He had eggs to gather, the milking to do...

But first the plowing.

ARTHUR'S BACK-TO-SCHOOL SURPRISE

开学第一天的尴尬

（美）马克·布朗　绘著

范晓星　译

CHISO 新疆青少年出版社

It was back-to-school time!

"I need this three-ring binder
and the Bionic Bunny pen,"
said Arthur.

"I need these big crayons,"
said D.W.

"And you both need new shoes,"
said Mom.

SHOES

Arthur liked the first pair
that he tried on.
D.W. tried on shoe after shoe.
"I like these," she said at last.

Then D.W. got a yellow coat
with a hood and lots of buttons.

Arthur got a blue jacket

with Red Sox written on it.

"I need a backpack,"

said Arthur.

He picked a Bionic Bunny one.

"I need one too," said D.W.

"You don't need backpacks

in nursery school," said Arthur.

"I need one to take

Mary Moo-Cow to school,"

she said.

"You can't take

that silly talking cow to school!"

said Arthur.

Mom sighed.

"Okay, D.W., pick one," she said.

D.W. picked one.

"Hey!"said Arthur. "It's the same as mine. You can't do that!"
"Why not?
I like Bionic Bunny too,"
said D.W.

Arthur picked up a backpack
with little ducks on it.
"This one is nice," he said.
"That's for babies," said D.W.
"I want Bionic Bunny."
Mom sighed.
"Oh, let her have it," she said.
"D.W. always gets her way,"
Arthur mumbled.

When they were leaving,

Mom saw a sign:

BOYS' UNDERPANTS SALE!

"You need some new underpants,"

she said, and held up a pair.

"Mom, please!" groaned Arthur.

Just then Francine stepped off

the escalator.

"Hi, Arthur," she giggled.

"Doing your

back-to-school shopping?"

Arthur was so embarrassed!

13

The first day of school,

Arthur put all of

his school things

into his backpack

and set it on the chair

by the back door.

D.W. put Mary Moo-Cow
into her backpack and set it on
the floor by the back door.

"We need to hurry," said Mom.

"Finish your breakfast
while I get the car."

"Arthur, can I see
your new classroom?" asked D.W.

"No way!" said Arthur.

"My friends will be there."

"Please," said D.W.

"N-O!Come on. We're late," he said.

17

Honk, honk went the car horn.

"Hurry up!" called Mom.

D.W. grabbed the backpack

on the chair

and ran out the door.

Arthur grabbed

the other backpack

and ran out too.

Arthur went to
his new classroom.
Most of his friends
were already there.
"Hi, Arthur," they said.
He unzipped his backpack
and out fell Mary Moo-Cow!
"School is fun!"
said Mary Moo-Cow.
"Can you spell fun?"

21

Everyone turned and
looked at Arthur.
They all laughed.
"Oh, look," said Muffy.
"Arthur brought
his favorite toy for show-and-tell!"
"Are you going to show us
your new underpants too?"
asked Francine.
Arthur covered his eyes.
He turned red.
He wished he could disappear.
Just then D.W. ran
into the classroom.

"Arthur, give me my backpack!

Here! I got yours by mistake,"

she giggled.

"And I got to see

  your new classroom.So there!"

"I'll get you for this!" said Arthur.

译文

3. 又要开学了！

"我要这个三环的文件夹，还有这支无敌超人兔的圆珠笔。"亚瑟说。

"我要这盒蜡笔。"朵拉说。

"你们两个都要买双新鞋。"妈妈回应。

4. 亚瑟只试了一双鞋，就说很喜欢。

朵拉试了一双又一双，最后才说："我喜欢这双。"

5. 朵拉还买了一件带帽子和小纽扣的黄色外衣。

亚瑟买了一件印着红袜队队标的蓝色夹克。

6. "我还要一个书包。"亚瑟说。他挑了无敌超人兔牌子的。

"我也要一个书包。"朵拉说。

"你才上幼儿园,不用背书包。"亚瑟提醒她。

"我要一个书包嘛,我要装我的小牛哞哞去上学。"朵拉哼哼唧唧地说。

"你不能带那个会说话的小牛去上学,傻乎乎的!"亚瑟回应。

8. 妈妈叹了口气说:
"好吧,朵拉,你挑一个吧。"
朵拉挑了一个。

9. "嘿!"亚瑟说,"这个书包和我的一样了。你不可以选它!"

"为什么不可以?我也喜欢无敌超人兔。"朵拉回答。

10. 亚瑟挑了一个有小鸭子图案的书包，说："瞧，这个多好看。"

"那是给小小孩的，"朵拉说，"我就要无敌超人兔。"

妈妈又叹了口气，说："好了，就让她选这个吧。"

"朵拉总是想要什么就能得到什么。"亚瑟小声咕哝。

12. 他们正要离开商店，妈妈抬眼看见一个宣传牌，上面写着：儿童内裤促销！

"你需要几条新内裤。"她边说边拿起一条。

"妈妈，求你了！"亚瑟嘟囔。

这时候，芳馨正好从电梯上走下来。

"嘿，亚瑟！"她咯咯笑起来，"你这是在开学大采购吗？"

亚瑟心里别提多难为情了。

14. 开学第一天，亚瑟把所有上学要用的东西都装进书包，然后把书包放在门后面的椅子上。

15. 朵拉把她的小牛哞哞也装进书包，把书包放在了门后面的地板上。

16. "我们得快点儿，"妈妈说，"我先去开车，快把你们的早饭吃完。"

"哥哥，我能到你的新教室去看看吗？"朵拉问。

"不行！"亚瑟回答，"我们班同学都在呢。"

"求你了！"朵拉说。

"不行！走吧，咱们要迟到了。"亚瑟回应。

18. 滴滴！汽车喇叭响了。

"快点！"妈妈大声喊。

朵拉抓起椅子上的书包跑出门去。

亚瑟抓过地板上的书包也跑出了门。

20. 亚瑟走进新教室，班里的同学都已经到齐了。

"嘿，亚瑟！"同学们招呼他。

亚瑟把书包拉链拉开，里面掉出来一只小牛！

"上学好开心！"小牛哞哞说，"你知道'开心'怎么写吗？"